MUCKABOUT
SCHOOL

Also by Ian Whybrow

www.littlewolf.co.uk

MUCKABOUT
SCHOOL

Ian Whybrow

Illustrated by Steve May

HarperCollins *Children's Books*

First Published in Great Britain by HarperCollins *Children's Books* in 2005
HarperCollins *Children's Books* is a division of HarperCollins*Publishers* Ltd,
77-85 Fulham Palace Road, Hammersmith, London W6 8JB

The HarperCollins *Children's Books* website address is:
www.harpercollinschildrensbooks.co.uk

1 3 5 7 9 8 6 4 2

Text copyright © Ian Whybrow 2005
Illustrations by Steve May 2005

ISBN 0 00 715876 9

The author and illustrator assert the moral right to be
identified as the author and illustrator of the work.

Printed and bound in England by
Clays Ltd, St Ives plc

The
Headmaster

MCUKABOU
SKOOl

$2+2=5$

Franky
Fearless

William
Whale

A NEW BOY AT MUCKABOUT

CHAPTER ONE

Gary Goody walked through the empty corridors of Muckabout School to his new classroom. He entered and stopped in his tracks.

"Oh no!" he thought. "I'm the first to arrive — again!"

He was just about to go back out to the playground when he heard a snort from behind the teacher's desk. It was Mr Dawdle just waking up from a nap. The lazy teacher straightened his sunglasses and stared straight at Gary.

"Gary!" Mr Dawdle groaned. "You're *early* again!"

Mr Dawdle dragged himself out of his comfortable armchair and stumbled over to where Gary was. In any other school, Mr Dawdle would have been a disgrace. He was as tall and skinny as a beanpole, with greasy hair scragged into a ponytail. His jeans and T-shirt were filthy and full of holes and he peered at Gary through sunglasses that were smeared with what looked like tomato ketchup.

"I'm sorry," sighed Gary.

"You should know the rules by now, yeah?" the teacher said, producing a biscuit from his pocket. He dusted the biscuit off and popped it into his mouth, chewing the biscuit as he yawned. "Well? What are they?" the teacher asked, spraying Gary with crumbs.

"Run in the corridors," Gary said.

"*Uh-huh*," said Mr Dawdle.

"Don't put up your hand. Be rude to teachers. Don't mind your manners. Always eat in class."

"And...?"

"...and never be on time," Gary said, quietly.

"Never be on time. Exactly, man. So what's so difficult? I haven't seen you run once, you're polite to everyone, you always say sorry and thank you (and please, come to think of it). And I haven't seen you eating anything in class all week."

"Sorry, sir," Gary replied.

"There you go again," Mr Dawdle grumbled. "You're just so... nice. You'll give Muckabout School a good name if you're not careful. It really isn't bad enough you know. Not bad enough at all. So maybe you should stay in at playtime and write the school motto one hundred times! Know what I mean?"

"Yes sir. Sorry sir."

"And cool it with the 'sorry' all the time, OK?"

CHAPTER TWO

Gary was such a good, well-behaved child that his anxious parents thought there must be something wrong with him. That's why they had sent him to Muckabout School. The "Muckabout Method" promised to make children happy and confident "through jollification and tomfoolery". Of course, that was really a fancy way of saying that it encouraged children to be naughty, but it sounded to Gary's mum and dad to be just the sort of thing Gary needed to make him a bit more normal.

The trouble was, Gary didn't really belong at Muckabout School. He just wasn't very good at… mucking about.

That's why at playtime on this, his fifth day at his new school, poor Gary felt it was his duty to stay indoors and write "Muckabout for ever!" until his arm ached. He glanced out of the window at the other children in the playground. They were having a great time playing football.

Franky Fearless, who kicked the ball again and again, might have scored if it wasn't for the giant William Whale, who blocked the goalmouth. Tim Tattle, the class stirrer, was encouraging Ricky Rude to pelt everyone with smelly mud. Whilst the others were busy, Wanda Offalot was quietly slipping out of the school gates.

Gary looked back at the lines he was writing.

"At least I'm getting into Mr Dawdle's good books," he thought.

It was ages before all the children came back into the classroom. They threw themselves on the floor in front of the telly. "Video, video, video, video!" they chanted.

Mr Dawdle smiled and opened the cupboard. "Alright, listen up, guys! You can have *The Revenge of Harry Potter, The Lord of the Rings Meets the Incredible Hulk, or Rugrats Go Mad in Jurassic Park*. Which do you fancy?"

He let them all have a good scream and shout about it. Then he noticed Gary bent over his desk at the back of the class. He was still writing, slowly and painfully doing the 'r' at the end of his ninety-ninth *Muckabout for ever*.

"Wait up a second, Gary!" called Mr Dawdle. "What's that you're doing?"

Gary blushed. He rose to his feet and made his way to the teacher's desk.

Mr Dawdle took the carefully written lines and frowned.

"Who told you to do this?" the teacher asked.

"You did sir," said Gary.

"I did? Oh Gary," Mr Dawdle sighed. "You didn't actually follow my orders, did you?"

"Yes sir," Gary replied.

"And this is your *best* writing, isn't it?" asked Mr Dawdle. "Proper, joined-up writing, with all the 't's crossed!"

"Yes, sir, sorry, sir," mumbled Gary.

"Oooo!" chorused the class. "Did you hear that, Mr Dawdle? He said he was sorry!"

"And he called you 'sir'," sneaked Tim Tattle.

"Gar-ee!" everyone groaned.

CHAPTER THREE

Try as he might, Gary just couldn't do anything right. He said his two-times table perfectly. He was the only child in the class who knew that fish were not mammals. And when Mr Dawdle asked his trick question – "Who wants to do some extra Geography?" – Gary was the one who fell for it. He looked really keen and nodded like mad.

"No, no, NO, Gary!" said Mr Dawdle. "NOBODY wants to do extra Geography!"

And just when he thought things couldn't get any worse, the chip fryer exploded.

The fact that the chip fryer exploded didn't bother Gary personally. He was much too good to eat anything as unhealthy as chips. But normal Muckabouts had chips with everything.

They had sausage and chips, fish and chips, burger and chips, chicken and chips, ice cream and chips, chocolate and chips, beans and chips, chips and chips… pretty much anything, so long as it was chips.

It was Mr Jolly, the headmaster, who delivered the bad news. He stood at the front of the class in a T-shirt that read:

LOVE FATTY FOOD HATE SPORT

"Muckabouts," Mr Jolly said in his most serious voice. "We are gathered here today to pay our respects to the school's chip fryer. I am sure many of you will have fine memories of that chip fryer. I know I have."

He sniffed and wiped his eye.

"But I am afraid that the poor thing exploded from over-use."

He lifted the hem of his T-shirt, exposing a hairy round tummy. He used the T-shirt to wipe his nose.

"Still – no point going hungry," Mr Jolly said, pulling his T-shirt back into place and patting his tummy. "It's packed lunches all round!"

The whole school cheered!

Quick as a flash, Mr Jolly produced a plastic raincoat and put it on, doing the zip up tight.

From all around the canteen there came the snap and hiss of violently shaken fizzy drink cans being opened. That was soon followed by the squeals and shrieks of dozens of young Muckabouts spraying one another with fountains of brightly coloured, sugary liquid.

The headmaster was ready. He pulled the hood of the raincoat over his head to protect his neck from getting too sticky whenever they tried to squirt him. To stop any of the sprayers getting too close, he screamed his war cry and pelted them with bread rolls.

Then, when the food fight was over, the children dug into their packed lunches.

Table by table, the noise changed to something like a regiment marching through deep gravel as all the children crunched away at their family-sized packets of crisps. That noise gave way in its turn to a gentle slurping as everyone began sucking the jam out of their doughnuts.

the BOSS

Everyone, that is, except... Gary Goody.

Gary always had a packed lunch, but

up until now he had managed to keep it a secret from everyone else. Now, as he prised the plastic lid off his lunchbox, it was finally revealed. He had a succulent red apple and neatly cut slices of carrot and celery. He had a luscious egg, mayonnaise and cress sandwich in seeded wholemeal bread. And to finish he had a low fat raspberry yoghurt.

Gary might have got away with it if he hadn't been sitting next to William Whale. William was such an enormous child that his bottom took up most of the bench on its own.

"ERRRR!" said William, as Gary crunched a stick of celery.

"I beg your pardon?" Gary asked.

"You can't eat that in here!" William wailed, rising to his feet. "That's healthy that is!"

At that, the whole table rose in protest. It wasn't long before Mr Jolly came over to see what was going on.

"Now what's all this?" Mr Jolly panted. "Have I missed another food fight?"

"Look what Gary's eating!" snitched Tim Tattle.

"Well I'm jiggered!" said Mr Jolly. "I've never seen anything like it! A lunchbox stuffed with food – and not a gram of extra sugar, salt, fat or preservative in sight! That is strictly against School Rules. Ha ha! You know what this means, sonny!"

Giggling happily, the headmaster reached a hand towards his top pocket. Out flipped… a red card.

"Off off off!" the Muckabouts chorused

merrily, as they tossed Gary in a tablecloth
and sprayed him with more fizzy drinks.

CHAPTER FOUR

The next morning, Gary stood outside the headmaster's office. His palms were sweating and his stomach was flipping like a pancake. He had never been so scared.

He knocked on the door, once, but there was no answer.

"You'll have to knock louder than that, dear," said Mrs Grunge, the school secretary. She lay on a sofa watching television, taking her pick from a large tray of chocolates in her lap.

Gary knocked again, louder this time.

"Come in," said a voice from inside.

When Gary entered, Mr Jolly leapt up from his chair and bounded around his desk to greet him. As he walked, the headmaster hitched the waistband of his trousers round his great round tummy. Then he tugged down his T-shirt, which read:

MCUKABOUT SKOOL

"Good to see you, Gary," the headmaster said, pointing to a chair for Gary to sit on whilst he leaned on his desk. "It seems like you've been having a bit of a tough time recently. You've not really got the hang of things around here, have you? Dashing into school early, minding your manners, eating healthily. I can see you're the sort of boy who likes to do up their top button and tuck their shirt in, but it's just not very… Muckabout. You must remember that at Muckabout School it's *bad* to be good. That's why your mum and dad were so keen for you to come here – to have some fun."

"I know," said Gary. "But I am trying. And I'm going to change! Honest I am."

"Well done, Gary. That's the spirit," laughed Mr Jolly. "You'll be a Muckabout before you know it."

"And I'm going to start right now,"

Gary said. And with that, he turned and walked very quickly out of the headmaster's office, past Mrs Grunge and all the way back to his own class.

Mr Dawdle was asleep in his comfortable armchair whilst the rest of the class played a game of indoor Frisbee.

Without pausing to say please or sir or thank you, Gary dashed to the white board and snatched up the red marker pen. In no time at all, he wrote the word BOTTOM in large, clear capitals.

"There!" he cried. "What do you think of that?"

One or two of the children started to clap, which woke Mr Dawdle.

"Not bad," the lazy teacher yawned. "Not bad at all. But did you *deliberately* spell that word correctly?"

Quick as a flash, Gary grabbed the

marker pen again and *scribbled*

BOTUM

in nasty, spidery letters.

"Well, it's a start, I suppose," Mr Dawdle said.

CHAPTER FIVE

The next week was an exciting one at Muckabout School. The workmen had come to build a new adventure playground next to the field and having the builders around was great fun. It meant that all the children would get a chance to show off and do even naughtier things than usual.

They got in the way of the men with the drills. They stood far too close to the diggers. They climbed over the safety barriers. They tripped over electric cables. They fell down holes. When they bothered to go into the classrooms, they trod mud everywhere.

Mr Jolly stood watching from his office window, laughing like mad. He was delighted with the children's behaviour. In fact, he was so pleased with one of the boys – Franky Fearless – that he called a special assembly.

Everybody bundled into the hall, pushing and shoving each other and making a tremendous noise. Mr Jolly smiled down from the edge of the stage. Today his T-shirt read:

DON'T WORRY
BE SILLY

He let the children fight and insult each other for a good while. Then he let them scrape their feet. Then he took a large paper bag from his pocket and blew into it once, twice, three times. When it was full of air, he twisted the end and burst the bag against his other hand.

All the children went "URGHHHH! HE GOT ME!"

They threw themselves down and pretended to be dead.

"Well done, Muckabouts!" yelled Mr Jolly. "That was *superbly* noisy and silly! But I expect you're wondering why you have to come in here and listen to boring old me. The answer is this. I've called you away from your normal fooling around for two reasons. "First, I wish to award Franky Fearless his Prefect's badge."

From the back of the hall came the rumble of small wheels on the wooden floor. Franky flashed down the central aisle of the hall on his skateboard, slapping people's hands as he passed. The infants squealed with delight as the young daredevil skidded to a halt and flipped the skateboard into his hand.

"I have watched a lot of mucking about on the building site during this past week, but Franky Fearless has easily been the most impressive," the headmaster continued. "Many of you thought of writing your names in the wet concrete, of course. Some of you left your footprints and handprints in it – but only Franky thought of throwing his whole body in and making a complete print of himself. So well done, Franky!"

"If only," thought Gary, who clapped as loudly as anyone. "If only I could think of something as clever as that."

There were loud and raucous cheers as Mr Jolly pinned a budge with the word **PREEFEK** on to Franky's T-shirt. Franky raised his skateboard above his head, acknowledging the applause.

"Second," the headmaster continued. "We've had two weeks at school this term and that's far too long. So we've all got to go away and have a week's holiday."

The school went crazy!

Everyone raced back to their classrooms to grab their bags.

Mr Dawdle was in the middle of his second nap that day when his class burst in.

"Just one thing before you go," Mr Dawdle yawned. "A little homework assignment."

Everyone groaned.

"Homework! No way!" screamed

Ricky Rude. He let out a ripping burp, just to remind everyone that he was the most revolting child in the class.

"Not proper homework, you doughnuts," said Mr Dawdle. "Whilst you're away, you've got to think of something *really* silly and mischievous to get up to when you come back. OK?"

The class looked at each other excitedly.

"And that means *everyone*," Mr Dawdle said. The whole class looked at Gary Goody. "And Gary – are you chewing something whilst I'm talking to you?"

"No, sir," said Gary. "Not me, sir!"

"Well why NOT?" asked Mr Dawdle. "Everybody else is!"

"But I don't have any gum, sir," Gary muttered.

"Just look under any table! There's bound to be plenty stuck there! And stop calling me sir!"

As the classroom emptied, Gary found himself alone. He was still picking bits of chewing gum from under the tables when Mr Jolly wandered past.

"Is that you, Gary?" the headmaster asked.

"Everyone else has gone," Gary explained. "I was collecting the chewing gum under the desks, just like Mr Dawdle said, but most of it's very hard. And it's got bits of fluff in it that get stuck in my teeth."

"Come on, Gary!" Mr Jolly said. "You're on holiday now! Why not run along and make a nuisance of yourself? There must be something bad you can do – something to make us all proud."

CHAPTER
SIX

All through the week, Gary tried to think of a plan that would make him a proper Muckabout, but the days passed and still he couldn't come up with anything. Being bad was just *not* something he was good at.

By the time he had to go back to school he still hadn't had one naughty thought.

Gary decided that the only thing to do was to get into the mood for mischief. So the night before school, he ate a whole packet of sticky toffees. When he woke in the morning, his stomach was growling and his teeth felt all wobbly.

And for some strange reason he also had a wicked plan.

When he arrived at school, the Muckabout infants were in the new Adventure Playground. You could tell by their shrill screams how much they were enjoying themselves.

Gary didn't go into class. Instead, he joined the infants and had a go on everything. He did loop the loop on the swings. He zoomed down the slides. He whizzed round the roundabout and threw himself off the bikes on springs. He hung like a monkey from the climbing frame and chased the infants through the rabbit tunnels.

He thought that the infants' teacher, Mrs Nevermind, and her classroom helper, Ms Moppup, might try to stop him. But Mrs Nevermind was going back and forth on one of the swings. And Ms Moppup was busy rubbing the infants' bumps when they fell off things. Gary had a brilliant time.

When he'd had enough, he picked out the sweetest, most angelic-looking, red-haired child. He crept up to her and whispered something in her ear.

It must have been something very funny, because she suddenly gave a great, big, wonderful smile.

When at last Gary drifted into the classroom, he was covered in dirt, his jacket and trousers torn. It was ten minutes to eleven.

"*Much* better, Gary!" beamed Mr Dawdle. "Apart from Wanda Offalot, who never comes in anyway, you're the last to arrive. Keep this up and you're going to be a star pupil at Muckabout School! The week off obviously did you some good. Did you come up with any ideas for mischief?"

"I've been practising cheek, Mister Dawdle the Fraudle!" shouted Gary.

"Wha… *what* did you say?"

"Ah, you must be deaf as well, Mister Squirmy Wormy Slowcoach!"

Mr Dawdle's mouth dropped open in amazement.

"And look out there, Mister Teachy Peachy Poo!" called Gary, pointing at the Adventure Playground.

The class stampeded over to look. They saw a sweet little girl with red hair and a round face stick a wide piece of sticking plaster over Ms Moppup's mouth. Meanwhile, some of the others tied her to the climbing frame with skipping ropes. The rest of the infants were busy squeezing Mrs Nevermind head first down a rabbit tunnel.

"That was all my idea!" Gary laughed.

CHAPTER SEVEN

By the middle of that week, Gary had done so many daft and dozy, massively mischievous things that Mr Jolly felt he had no choice. He simply had to give him Muckabout School's highest honour.

All the staff and children came to a special assembly. They gasped with admiration as the Head listed Gary Goody's mischievous tricks.

"It's hard to say which was your best trick, Gary," Mr Jolly cooed. "Removing the doorknobs? Eating all your crayons? Filling the cushions in the staff room with conkers? We loved them all, but my favourite was when you wrote TRUBBLE on the side of a dustbin, filled it with custard, and jumped in. Now that is what I call *getting into trouble* in a very clever way!"

Gary punched the air in triumph. "MUCKABOUT FOR EVER!" he yelled.

The whole school joined in, chanting and screaming. Even Franky Fearless whistled his respect.

"Step up on to the stage, Gary," said Mr Jolly.

With a thumping heart, Gary did as he was told. The headmaster shook his hand warmly and into the other he pressed Muckabout School's greatest award.

The words on Gary's special badge, embroidered in gold, read:

Gary had never felt more proud or more excited.

But then he made a big mistake: a dreadful mistake that ruined everything. How could he have been so stupid? If only he could stop the clock and wind it back. But it was too late! Out popped those terrible words and there was no taking them back.

HED BOY MUKABOUT SCHULE

"Thank you very much indeed, sir!" he cried.

★

Mr Jolly's letter to Gary's parents, explaining why Gary had been expelled, was unusually stern.

Gary's mother shook her head sadly as she read out the letter to her husband at the breakfast table. For a little while, Gary had been so much more fun. They had really thought he was getting somewhere.

Dear Mr and Mrs Goody,

I am sorry to tell you that your son, Gary, has been permanently excluded from Muckabout School because of his persistently decent and polite behaviour. He broke many of our school rules, including:

Let your litter lie
Pockets are for hands
and
Don't bother – it's only a lesson

It is true that during this last
week, your Gary made some effort to
fit in and be a normal, naughty
young Muckabout. But it seems that
this was all on the surface. I regret to
inform you that underneath, he is
hopelessly, incurably GOOD.

Yours truly,

I. M. Jolly
Head teacher

MUCKABOUT OUTING

CHAPTER ONE

It was midday on Thursday morning and Mr Jolly the headmaster had decided to call it a day.

He flipped the on-switch on the intercom on his desk and sent his voice out over the speakers to all classes. "Sorry to interrupt you, Muckabouts, but most of you have been in school for a couple of hours, so you might as well trot off now and enjoy a nice long weekend. Bye bye! And teachers and support staff, would you mind popping into the staff room on your way home for a quick meeting?"

Cheers from the kids.

Boos from the staff.

Like water down the plughole, the children of the world's silliest school swirled and gurgled out of the gates. Only a few unlucky ones remained, stuck in the lavatories because one of the infants had pasted the toilet seats with glue.

In the staff room the headmaster handed out sweeties to cheer the teachers up. On his T-shirt was printed:

DON'T SCRATCH YOUR HEAD FEED HIM

"Right, everybody," he smiled. "We all want to put our feet up, don't we? Ha ha! So let's get this over with as soon as possible. Item one on the agenda. Gary Goody. As you know, his parents have begged us to give him another chance. And the Local Education Authority says that all the other schools in the area are full, so it seems that the boy is now with us permanently."

"Oh dear, not to worry!" cooed Mrs Nevermind, the infants' teacher.

"It's alright for you," said Mr Dawdle, the lazy junior teacher. "You don't have to have him in your class."

"Let's move on to item two," said the Head. "The school outing. As I think you all know, *The Daily Spoilsport* has been trying to ban Muckabout School from going on its annual school outing ever since our trip to Sewage-on-Sea."

"Well they did have to call the lifeboat out three times," murmured Ms Moppup, the classroom assistant for the infants.

"And I was on the office phone for three weeks afterwards dealing with the complaints from other passengers on the train," said Mrs Grunge the school secretary.

"I don't think many of you will forget the news story," Mr Jolly said, producing a copy of *The Daily Spoilsport*.

He held it up for everyone to see.

THE SPOILSPORT SAYS:
STOP MUCKABOUT OUTINGS!

"It says that our pupils were 'noisy, bad mannered and a public menace'," Mr Jolly read out.

Underneath was a large picture of a small, freckle-faced child on a skateboard. He was letting fly with a squeezy bottle of tomato sauce at a line of startled people. The caption for the picture was: "Sauce Terror Strikes at Seaside!"

The teachers giggled.

"Yeah, man, that's Franky Fearless. He's in my class," Mr Dawdle drawled proudly. "He's the coolest, daftest, cheekiest young daredevil in the whole school."

"And it was a lovely shot, you know," added Mrs Nevermind. "Those people were quite a way away."

"Wonderful stuff!" the headmaster beamed. "Absolutely wonderful. Young Franky Fearless is a thoroughly Muckabout sort of chap. Just the sort of high-spirited individual we like to encourage here. I think we owe it to him and others like him to enjoy another educational visit as soon as possible. So you'll all be delighted to know I've ordered a coach for next Tuesday, ha ha!"

"Where to?" asked Mr Dawdle.

"To the zoo, of course!" cried the Head.

"The zoo!" chorused the staff.

"I just love zoos," the headmaster said. "Marvellous places. Perfect for outings."

"But, Headmaster, everyone knows the zoo's on its last legs," said Ms Moppup. "They're struggling to keep the place going. Wouldn't a visit from our kids be… you know… *tough* on them? I mean, what with the publicity we've been getting in the *Spoilsport*, a visit by Muckabout might… well… finish the zoo off?"

"Come to think of it," said Mrs Grunge, "Another story in the *Spoilsport* might finish the school off too."

Mr Jolly's eyes took on a mysterious and mischievous gleam.

"The trip to the zoo will go ahead as planned. Next Tuesday!" he boomed. "It will be a marvellous educational opportunity for our children and a roaring success for everyone concerned. You mark my words!"

CHAPTER TWO

The following Tuesday – Outing Day –
Mr Dawdle and Mrs Nevermind were not
at all pleased. Crowds of children had
actually had the cheek to turn up,
including *all* the infants. More pupils
meant more work – something that
neither of them wanted to worry about.

Gary Goody was the first to arrive.
Then William Whale rolled up, followed
by Ricky Rude and Tim Tattle. Even
Wanda Offalot, the girl who held the

school record for bunking off, had come along.

"Now it looks like we're stuck with a whole coach-load," moaned Mr Dawdle. "Still, Franky Fearless hasn't turned up. That might save us a bit of trouble. Do any of you guys know where Franky is?"

"I know!" said Tim Tattle, who was always snitching and stirring. "You know he thinks he's a brilliant skateboarder? Well, I bet Franky that he couldn't do a headstand on a skateboard. Wearing a blindfold."

"So what happened?" said Mr Dawdle.

"He did it," said Tim. "But his silly old leg got bust."

"Oh dear," twittered Mrs Nevermind. "Poor boy! Still, never mind. At least he's got another one."

Just then the coach arrived.

The coach driver, who had driven the

Muckabouts to Sewage-on-Sea the year before, was ready for them this time. Instead of coming into the schoolyard he parked opposite the gates. He was wearing body armour and a helmet, and he approached the playground with a loudspeaker and an angry-looking dog on a chain.

"MOVE IN AN ORDERLY FASHION TOWARDS THE COACH," the driver boomed.

"DO NOT ON ANY ACCOUNT ATTEMPT TO BOARD THE COACH BEFORE PASSING THROUGH THE MOBILE SECURITY BARRIER!"

The dog snarled and gathered the Muckabouts into a nervous flock.

The driver made everyone file through his X-ray machine. He confiscated chewing gum, flour bombs, bad eggs, catapults and water pistols.

When William Whale stepped towards him out of the crowd, the driver spotted an orange stain at the top of the boy's trousers that was starting to spread towards his knees.

"What have you got in your pocket?" the driver asked, suspiciously.

"Spaghetti hoops," explained William, who hated going anywhere without a little snack.

"Well make sure it doesn't leak on my seats," the driver said.

Poor old Muckabouts! There was nothing to do on the boring thirty-minute journey except do rude signs at passing drivers.

So Tim Tattle decided to stir things up a bit.

He was sitting next to Ricky Rude, the most revolting child in the whole of Muckabout School. William Whale was sitting just across the aisle, the spaghetti hoops in his trouser pocket starting to puddle on to the floor.

"Look, Ricky," stirred Tim, pointing at the puddle. "What does it remind you of?"

Quick as a change of traffic lights, Ricky turned green and reached for a sick bag, not knowing that Tim had snipped the bottom off for a joke. Up came Ricky's breakfast... and splooshed all over his shoes.

That set off a couple of the infants who threw up in turn.

"Well played, Ricky!" yelled Tim. "Nice one, William!"

"ERRRRR!" all the Muckabouts screamed.

CHAPTER THREE

As the smell of sick wafted through the coach, the driver became more and more desperate to get to the zoo and get rid of his passengers. To make things worse, other drivers had started beeping at him with their horns when they passed, and behind the coach a steady stream of cars slowly turned into a traffic jam.

"It could just be the kids making rude signs out of the window," he thought, but the traffic continued to snake behind him, the drivers waving and beeping their horns. By the time he arrived at the zoo, a police car and two police motorbikes escorted him, their sirens blaring.

The coach driver brought the coach to a halt outside the zoo gates and jumped straight out, kissing the first policeman he saw.

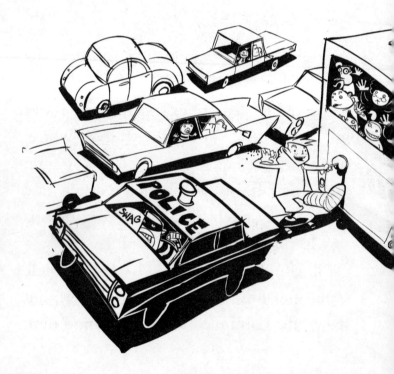

Out of the coach poured the Muckabouts and round to the back of the coach they ran. The coach driver followed them, fearing the worst.

But all they found was an angelic-looking boy on the back of a skateboard.

"Is this one of yours?" the coach drive asked Mr Dawdle.

"It's Franky Fearless!" Mr Dawdle replied. "But how did you get there, Franky?"

"I borrowed my dad's sink plunger, stuck it on the back of the coach and got myself a tow on my skateboard," explained Franky.

"*Wow!* And with a broken leg plastered up to the thigh!" gasped Mr Dawdle.

"Yeah, well, I've still got another one!" laughed Muckabout School's very own mini daredevil.

Whilst everyone was congratulating Franky, the police were talking to the coach driver, who was now crying with relief. It was quite a picture.

CLACK! went a camera in a nearby bush.

CHAPTER FOUR

When the Muckabouts finally made it to the gates of the zoo, they found a sad-looking banner that read:

WHAT CAN YOU DO TO HELP SAVE MANKEY ZOO?

"Having problems?" Mr Dawdle asked the man in the ticket office.

The man looked embarrassed. "We'd be all right if we had a few more visitors," he said. "People just don't seem interested any more. And it's having a bad effect on the animals too. We've got lions that just lie about. The gorilla sits in the corner of his cage and sulks. The seals haven't got the heart to put on a show at feeding time and the monkeys can't be bothered with anything. And did I mention our boa constrictor? He's gone off his food altogether! The zoo's just no fun any more."

"Bad news, man," said Mr Dawdle.

"Still, not to worry!" twittered Mrs Nevermind. "Our kiddies will soon liven things up for you, I'm sure!"

Mr Dawdle paid everyone's entrance fee and all the Muckabouts poured through the gate to the four corners of the zoo.

All, that is, except Gary Goody. He had politely waited for everyone else to go in before him and stood chatting to the man in the ticket booth.

"I love animals," he told the man. "I can't wait to go inside and look around. I've even started writing some animal poems. My latest work is called *My Fluffy Little Kitty*. Would you like me to recite it to you?"

"That's very kind of you, sonny," said the ticket man. "But I've got a few things on my mind at the moment."

"It won't take long," Gary said. But at that moment Gary heard a strange noise coming from the bushes.

"Psstt!"

Gary turned around, but there was nobody there.

He was just about to go through the gates when he heard the same sound again: "Psstt!"

Then out of the bushes behind him emerged a man with a long, pointy nose and a camera with a very long lens.

"Who are you?" Gary asked.

"Ken Keen," the man said. "I'm a reporter with the *Spoilsport*."

"How exciting!" Gary said. "I would love to be a writer. In fact, I've just finished a poem called *My Fluffy Little Kitty*. Would you like me to recite it to you?"

"Later," the reporter interrupted. "Here's the deal. I'll make sure one of your fluffy poems gets published in the paper…"

Gary squealed with delight.

"…if you give me the names and background information about anyone we see from Muckabout School," the man continued.

"Are you doing an article then?" asked Gary.

"Yeah," the reporter said. "Nice piece about the zoo and the school – 'A Wonderful Educational Day Out' – that sort of thing."

"What a good idea," Gary said. "It would be an honour!"

CHAPTER FIVE

The man in the ticket office had said that the lions just lay about, so Gary was surprised to hear exciting noises as he and Ken Keen approached the lions' enclosure.

They heard ferocious roars, cheers, clapping and shouts of what sounded like "O-Lay!". Quite a crowd had gathered.

Gary and Ken squeezed through to the front. Deep down in the pit below were two small figures. One of them, Wanda

Offalot, was busy barbecuing the lions' meat. The smaller child, a freckled boy with one leg in plaster up to the thigh, was distracting the furious lion by waving his skateboard about.

The crowd gasped and some even fainted as the lion crouched. With a horrible roar, the lion sprang at the unflinching little daredevil.

"I know that kid!" snarled Ken Keen. "That's the little terror who played havoc at Sewage-on-Sea! He's the one I caught on camera before! What's the little loony's name?"

"That's Franky Fearless," smiled Gary. "He's a school prefect."

As he watched, Franky whipped off his T-shirt, jumped on to his skateboard and gave it a push with his good leg. That sent him whizzing along the edge of the enclosure like a rider on the wall of death.

He passed within inches of the snapping jaws of the lion, twirling his vest like a bullfighter's cape. The lion span giddily and bit thin air.

"O-Lay!" yelled the crowd. "Look at that kid go!"

CLACK! Went Ken Keen's camera.

It took a while to find Chesty the

gorilla. Surprisingly, after what the ticket man had said, there was quite a crowd watching him, too.

"That's odd," said Gary. "What could be interesting about a large primate sulking in a corner?"

Once more, Gary and Ken Keen pushed through to the front. A huge gorilla was heaving and straining at the bars of his cage. He seemed to be trying to rip them open so that he could get at a skinny little monkey hopping up and down just outside.

With a shriek of tearing metal, the bars gave way.

"Great Scott!" exclaimed Ken Keen. "It's a break-out!"

The crowd screamed, "Look out! Run for it! The gorilla's escaping!"

But no. The gorilla wasn't coming out. The monkey was going in.

And boy, did the monkey have fun with his new chum!

The gorilla and the monkey started with a chest-thumping competition.

Then they did whoo-hooing and see-how-many-bananas-you-can-stuff-into-your-mouth. That was followed by flea-exploring and then wrestling.

Unfortunately, Chesty the gorilla, not knowing his own mighty strength, ripped off the poor little monkey's head.

"Ooooooooo!" screamed the crowd, as they closed their eyes in horror.

But when everyone uncovered their eyes they saw that the monkey had not been beheaded after all.

Instead, Chesty was happily playing football with the head from a monkey *suit*.

And urging him to try to score a goal, with his freckled face plain for all to see was… Franky Fearless.

CLACK! went Ken Keen's camera.

"Gotcha!" the reporter said with a smug twist on his ratty face. "This is enough to put him behind bars for good."

"What's that, Mr Keen?" asked Gary, who was still clapping Franky Fearless.

"Nothing for you to worry about, laddy," the reporter said. "Where to next?"

Gary was keen to see the Reptile House,

so the cunning reporter went with him.

There they found a group of people watching with fascination as the boa constrictor bulged and writhed. It had an enormous lump in its middle.

Tim Tuttle was among the spectators. He turned to Gary and said, "That's William Whale in there. He was trying to feed it hot dogs and it ate him."

"Isn't that fascinating?" said Gary, turning to Ken Keen. "You see the boa constrictor has a remarkable digestive system…"

CLACK! went Ken Keen's camera. CLACK! CLACK! CLACK!

CHAPTER SIX

"I think this zoo is rather fun, in spite of what the man in the ticket office said, don't you, Mr Keen?" said Gary. "You will say nice things about it in your article, won't you?"

"Yeah yeah," panted Ken Keen, whose mind was on the headline he was going to write. He was trying to decide which word to put in bigger letters: **SHOCK** or **HORROR**? He was also wondering whether he could get just one more picture

– this time with *lots* of Muckabouts.

"What happened to all the little ones from your school?" Ken Keen asked.

"There are the twins," said Gary, pointing to a girl and a boy from the infants. They stood in the Petting Park among the goats, bunny rabbits and guinea pigs.

"How sweet," said Gary. "Shall we go and say hello?"

But as they approached, they noticed that the children were picking up things from the ground: smelly brown pellets dropped by the goats and bunnies.

"What are you going to do with those?" asked Ken Keen.

The twins looked up and answered together.

"We're going to put them into dad's muesli," they grinned.

CLACK! went Ken Keen's camera.

"Who's looking after you lot then?" asked Ken Keen.

"Mrs Nevermind is looking round the gift shop," the twins chorused. "And Mr Dawdle said he was going to have a lie down."

"And where are the other infants?"

The twins simply pointed towards the Monkey House.

Ken Keen swung his nose in the

direction of the vast expanse of the Monkey House. At first, his attention was taken by the visitors standing around the huge cage. They were throwing things – food it seemed. They threw peanuts and fruit, cakes and chocolates, through the bars. They were clearly enchanted by the little wild things inside.

Some of the little creatures filled their cheeks with food, whilst others chased each other round and swung wildly from branch to branch. Others held out their hands or rattled the wire, or scratched their armpits and made funny faces.

"Mrs Nevermind's infants!" Gary cried.

The infants were so brilliant at monkey business that even the monkeys started laughing and chattering and joining in. The crowd watching roared their approval.

CLACK! went Ken Keen's camera. Ken Keen could hardly believe his luck. A gang of small children running riot – and not a teacher in sight. This was too easy.

"What's next?" he asked excitedly.

"We could try the seals," Gary suggested.

But when they got there, things didn't look promising.

The seals flopped sleepily on rocks. A keeper stepped through a gateway at the back and trudged on to a little platform that took him out over the water. He banged the sides of the bucket with his knuckles and called out, "Here we go, my dears. Come to daddy. Fetch a little fishy for daddy!" He reached into the bucket and flipped a herring high into the air. The seals gazed blankly at the keeper. Not one of them moved.

But before the fish hit the water, a shape flew out of the sky from the edge of the lake.

It appeared at terrific speed from among the greenery on the far bank. There was a flash of skateboard wheels, a loud bark of pleasure and a snap of teeth, followed by a satisfying SPLOOOSH as the shape caught the fish and bombed into the murky water.

"What was THAT?" yelled the keeper.

"That looked to me like Franky Fearless!" Gary gasped.

The little daredevil leapt out of the water like a dolphin. The seals barked their pleasure and the crowd roared.

"Did you get that, Mr Keen?" asked Gary. "Mr Keen?"

He turned to see Ken Keen hurrying away.

"I got it alright!" he hissed, pulling out his mobile phone.

"Chief? Hold the front page!" the sneaky reporter yelled. "I've got some sensational pictures here for you – and a story that might just finish off Mankey Zoo and Muckabout School – for ever!"

"Oh, dear!" sighed Gary. "What have I done?"

CHAPTER SEVEN

Gary got up early to read the newspaper next morning.

What he saw upset him so much that he hid the newspaper from his mum and dad and stayed in bed all day with a headache.

"That Ken Keen is such a rotter!" he complained to himself. "I felt sure he would write a nice story about the zoo. Now I'm going to be in such trouble. And he hasn't even published my poem."

But the next day, Gary had decided that he must go into school, even if it was for the last time. He knew Mr Jolly would be furious with him for helping the *Spoilsport*. The school inspectors were probably already there, closing the school down. And what was going to happen to the poor defenceless zoo?

As expected, as soon as Gary arrived at school, Mr Jolly grabbed him and rushed him into his study. Mr Jolly's T-shirt, on this blackest of days, read:

MCUKABOUT 4EVA!

Other pupils from the junior school were already in the headmaster's office. There was Franky Fearless and Ricky Rude, Tim Tattle and even William Whale (looking a little nibbled around the edges). Next to them stood Mr Dawdle and Mrs Nevermind. They were all crowding around the Thursday edition of the *Spoilsport*, which was spread out on the headmaster's desk. They must all be in serious trouble.

But then Gary stepped a little closer and read the headline:

NEW DAWN FOR ZOO THAT GOES MUCKABOUT

"You mean they're not closing the zoo down?" asked Gary.

"Not a hope of it!" the headmaster chortled.

"And what about Muckabout?"

"Muckabout's *for ever*, Gary," Mr Jolly beamed. "Remember that! And I think that we can count our visit to the zoo as Muckabout's most successful outing ever! The school gets special mention in the paper today for making the zoo 'an exciting and entertaining place'! What's more, the *Spoilsport* had loads of complaints yesterday from visitors who *loved* their day at the zoo, saying that Ken Keen's report was unfair. The result is – he's been given the push, ha ha! And young Franky here has even been offered a free lifetime pass. Look, today's paper is full of stuff about the plucky little chap who doesn't allow a broken leg to stop him having fun!"

"But what about me?" asked Gary. "I feel terrible about helping that rotter, Ken Keen."

"Not a bit of it – not a bit of it. Tim Tattle told us all about what you've been up to. First rate snitching all round! I said when I planned this outing that it would be a roaring success for everybody concerned, and I was right! Now who's for a drink of something tooth-rottingly fizzy and a slice of chocolate cake?"

Gary was so relieved that he quite forgot himself. He stuffed a huge piece of cake into his mouth, washed it down with a glass of fizzy pop and shouted at the top of his voice: "MUCKABOUT FOR EVER!"

Witch-in-Training
Flying Lessons

Maeve Friel

Illustrated by Nathan Reed

On Jessica's tenth birthday she discovers that she is a witch! With Miss Strega as her teacher, and a broomstick to fly, Jessica is ready to begin her training. The first book in a magical series.

ISBN 0 00 713341 3

HarperCollins *Children's Books*

★ MICHAEL
MORPURGO

ILLUSTRATED BY GRIFF

When Jackie finds a broken garden gnome in a
rubbish skip, she is determined to make him as good
as new. In return, Mister Skip makes Jackie's wishes
come true... almost! A fairy-tale for today from a
master storyteller.

ISBN 0 00 713474 6

HarperCollins *Children's Books*